Disney

Hannah Montana

The Essential Guide

Robby Ray Stewart
Jackson Stewart

Written by Beth Landis Hester

CONTENTS

Hannah Montana

RICO'S
RICO'S

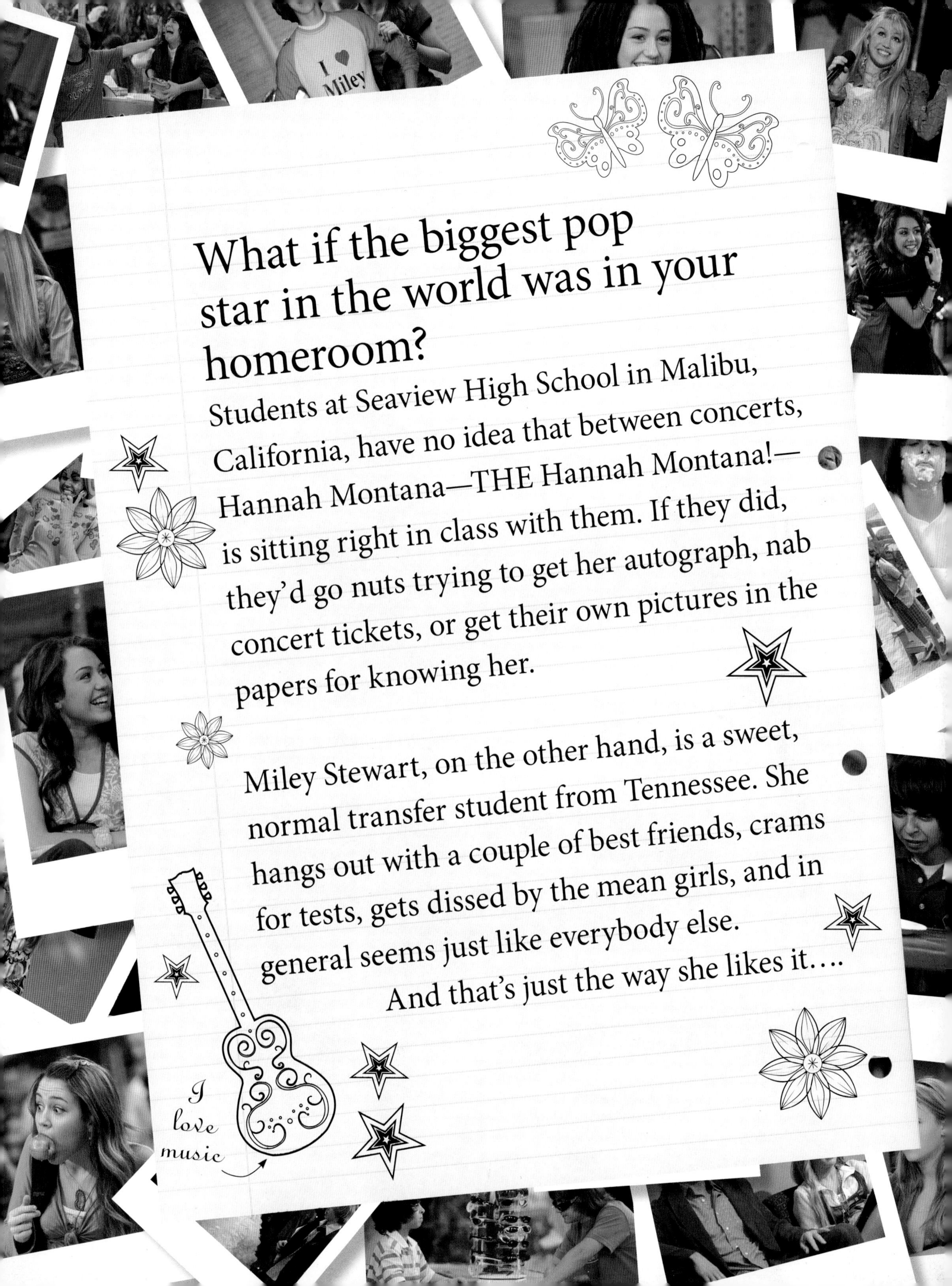
I ♥ Miley
What if the biggest pop star in the world was in your homeroom?
Students at Seaview High School in Malibu, California, have no idea that between concerts, Hannah Montana—THE Hannah Montana!—is sitting right in class with them. If they did, they'd go nuts trying to get her autograph, nab concert tickets, or get their own pictures in the papers for knowing her.
Miley Stewart, on the other hand, is a sweet, normal transfer student from Tennessee. She hangs out with a couple of best friends, crams for tests, gets dissed by the mean girls, and in general seems just like everybody else.
And that's just the way she likes it….
I love music

GIRL NEXT DOOR

Underneath the glitz and glamour of Hannah Montana is a small-town girl from Tennessee, just trying to fit in at California's Seaview High. To the kids at school, Miley Stewart is a normal kid—with homework, curfews, and embarrassing moments, to boot.

Cute clothes aren't just for pop stars! Miley's wardrobe includes sweet skirts, colorful tops, comfy ballet flats, and even some outrageous hats.

DOWNTIME

Life as a regular kid means getting to dress down, chill out, and enjoy quiet time. For Miley, weekend mornings at home are all about taking it slow and kicking back in her PJs.

"I'm just like everybody else."

MILEY'S TOP 5

things about being a normal kid

- High school!
- **Having down-to-earth friends**
- Not having to deal with paparazzi
- **Peace and quiet walking down the street**
- Being accepted for who you really are

A SWEET NOTE

Music was a way of life in the Stewart house even before Hannah Montana started climbing the charts. Miley can play piano and guitar, and loves singing with her dad, Robby Ray.

Miley's natural hair color is a pretty brown.

A cuddle with Beary Bear always cheers Miley up when she's nervous or sad. He's been with her since she was three—and if anyone knows the perils of living with Miley's brother Jackson, it's Beary!

A NORMAL KID

She may not have tons of adoring fans, but Miley Stewart has the things that really count: true friends, a supportive family, and the chance to enjoy growing up. At school, Miley gets good grades and lots of love from her friends, even if the popular girls pass her over. At home, she's Daddy's little girl.

Bright colors and girly skirts are just Miley's style.

DID YOU KNOW? The smell of raspberries makes Miley sick!

California kids Oliver Oken and Lilly Truscott are Miley's BFFs. They love surfing, chilling out at the beach, and hanging out with Miley!

FACTFILE: Miley Stewart

Nicknames: Miles, Bud, Smiley Miley, Stinky Stewart

Catchphrases: "Sweet niblets!," "Say what?," "Ya think?," "Good to know."

Favorite things: Beary Bear, music, shopping, hanging out with friends

Secret talents: Singing, getting good grades, sleepwalking, dancing the tango

SECRET STAR

Hannah's number-one rule for fans at her concerts? Get up and dance! She likes her fans to reach out and get involved in the show.

Hannah Montana is a teenage pop sensation! She lives the high life with fabulous parties, limousines, and a slammin' wardrobe—but her favorite thing is getting to perform her music. Wherever she goes, fans and photographers follow. It's a crazy life…and Hannah Montana rocks it!

"Are you ready to rock?"

ROCKIN' ROLE MODEL

Hannah Montana knows her fans look up to her, and does her best to set a good example. She volunteers her time in telethons, benefit concerts, and reading to kids at local schools. She tries to inspire her fans to be honest, brave, and kind.

LIVE IN CONCERT!

Hannah Montana's sold-out concerts are a special treat for fans. With choreographed dances, quick costume changes, pyrotechnics, video screens, and lots of great songs, they're a lot of work for Hannah Montana and her crew—but it's worth it!

HANNAH'S TOP 5

things about being a pop star

- Sharing her music with all her fans
- **Working with amazing people**
- Visiting different countries
- **Expressing her own style**
- Being a role model

PUBLIC FACE

Even superstars have to deal with life's problems—on a billboard-size scale! But Hannah Montana doesn't hide her flaws; she shows her fans that she's a real person, zits and all.

FACTFILE: Hannah Montana

Nicknames: America's songbird, Princess of Pop

Catchphrases: "Sweet niblets!," "Say what?," "Ya think?"

Favorite things: Performing, meeting fans, answering Hannah Montana's advice column

Secret talents: Playing tennis, hawking cannoli, raising money for charity

BEST OF BOTH WORLDS

Miley Stewart's double identity is a big part of her life...and Hannah Montana's music. "The Other Side of Me," "Just Like You," "Rock Star," and "The Best of Both Worlds" riff on the theme without giving away the secret.

Hannah Montana is a pro at smiling for the cameras—whether she's playing nice with her rival Mikayla or playing hard on the tennis courts.

A rhinestone-heart buckle sweetens up Hannah's edgy outfit.

THE SWITCH

Hannah Montana is a pro at working the stage…and Miley Stewart is a pro at changing into Hannah Montana! She makes the complicated switch—from regular girl to glamour girl in no time flat—look easy thanks to lots of practice, some help from her friends, and her secret weapons: accessories and make up supplies.

Underneath it all…is Miley Stewart: brunette, fresh-faced, relaxed, and dressed to chill.

2

eye make up

Blue eyes are defined with eye shadow, eye liner, and mascara.

Miley has an array of eye shadow colors for every occasion.

Pearly white teeth make for a winning smile.

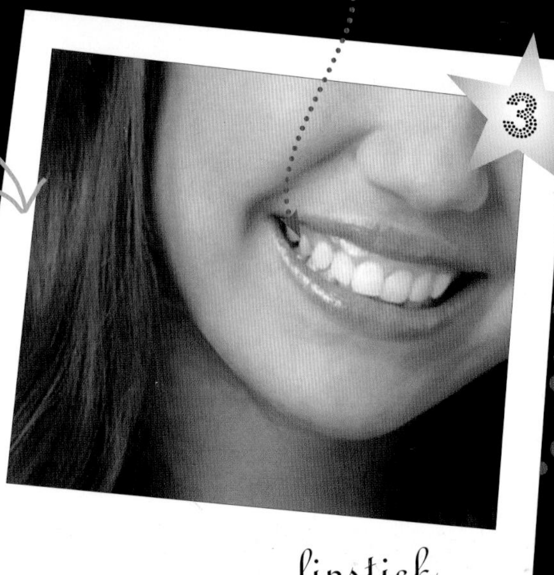

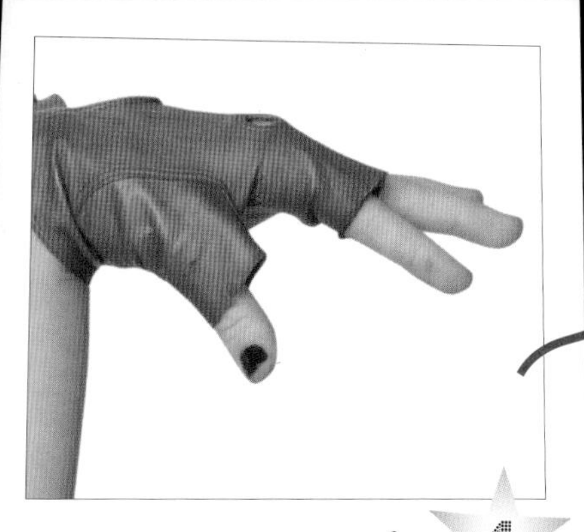

nail polish 4

The secret to a complete transformation is attention to detail–fingernails included!

5 jewelry

Necklaces, bracelets, and earrings add shimmer and shine.

blonde wig 6

7 boots zipped up

Her blonde wig is trademark Hannah Montana.

IT'S HANNAH TIME!

By showtime, Hannah Montana is warmed up, dressed up, and, well, Hannah Montana! Miley's got to act fast to get her look right, from kickin' boots to Hannah's famous blonde hair.

8 Hannah Montana

Robby is always ready with an open ear and down-home advice. When life gets tough for Miley, a good talk with her dad is often the best medicine.

ROBBY RAY

Robby Ray Stewart is the most important person in Miley and her brother Jackson's lives, and he's proud of it! He's a stay-at-home dad who puts his kids—and Hannah Montana's career—first. But that doesn't mean it's easy for him to watch his little girl grow up.

FAMILY FIRST

In a family that includes Jackson, Miley, and Hannah Montana too, being a dad is a full-time job! Robby makes life in the Stewart house lots of fun—but he also tries to teach his kids good values with a sense of humor, creative advice, and even the occasional prank.

It takes time, and some sweet-smelling gel to get hair this good!

Robby writes all of Hannah's songs on his old guitar.

MEMORIES OF MOM

Miley's mom died before Hannah Montana became a star, but she always believed in Miley's talent. The memories of her love inspire Miley to follow her dream.

"Yeeee dawgy!"

FATHER KNOWS BEST

With two teenage kids, Robby knows a thing or two about keeping the peace. He finds creative ways to help Miley and Jackson work out their differences—from sharing a bathroom to duking it out as sumo wrestlers!

It's hard for Robby to see his babies grow up—especially Miley, whose life as Hannah Montana includes traveling all over the country. He tries to keep her close, but also knows it's time to start letting her live her own life.

ROXY'S GOT HER EYES ON YOU!

When Robby hired Roxy to protect Hannah Montana, he got more than a bodyguard. Roxy is tough, over-protective, and looks after Miley and Jackson like they're her own kids. She's the only one Robby trusts to babysit when he's away.

TOP SECRET IDENTITY

Before Robby's days as daddy to Jackson and Miley, he was the Stewart on stage. His fans loved his songs like "I Want My Mullet Back," and called him the "Honky-Tonk Heartthrob." These days, he uses fake mustaches ("Uncle Earl" and "Aunt Pearl") as a disguise when he's in public as Hannah Montana's manager and songwriter.

The Honky-Tonk Heartthrob

ROBBY RAY'S TOP 5

parenting tips

- **Start each day with breakfast and a song**
- Keep a sense of humor
- **Make time to talk—and listen**
- Don't be afraid to let your kids grow up
- **Don't forget who the top dawg is!**

THE JACKSONATOR

Jackson Stewart is two years older than his sister Miley, but he's not exactly the mature big-brother type. He'd rather goof off than study, fill out college applications, or clean his room. But when it comes to getting out of trouble, he pulls out all the stops!

When Jackson sets his mind to something—like auditioning for Teen Wilderness Challenge*—he throws himself into it with a roar!*

Surfer-dude beads are just right for the beach life.

CHILLAX!

Jackson cracks himself up with corny jokes—laughs and good times are what he's all about. He never takes himself too seriously, and isn't afraid to be embarrassed for a good cause: impressing girls, earning some extra cash, or protecting Miley's secret.

Jackson sports cool cotton shirts in bright colors.

FACTFILE: Jackson Rod Stewart

Nicknames: The Jacksonator

Catchphrases: "Oooh, yeah," "Dad, I tried to stop her!," "She did it!," "Good day. I said good day!"

Likes: Food, girls, watching sports, video games, sugar, chocolate bunnies

Secret talents: Volleyball, belching contests, ping-pong, jumping on a pogo stick

BIG BROTHER

Jackson and Miley butt heads sometimes, and he isn't always crazy about Miley and Hannah Montana hogging the spotlight. But when push comes to shove, Jackson is proud of his little sister and is there to support her when she needs him—even if it means dressing up in crazy costumes to help her get out of trouble.

"Even my moves have moves."

WORKING MAN

Jackson mans the counter at Rico's Surf Shop, selling hot dogs and drinks to the beach crowd. Rico, whose dad owns the shop, is a tiny tyrant of a boss—but at least the job lets Jackson hang out with friends while he works.

JACKSON'S TOP 5

money-making schemes

- **Dishing out cheese jerky at the beach**
- Selling Hannah Montana's used tissues online
- **Collecting Robby Ray's spare change**
- "Fixing" the kitchen sink
- **Modeling Hannah Montana's outfits for fittings**

It takes extreme measures to get a son like Jackson to clean the kitchen or replace the toilet paper! But he hates to see his dad disappointed—so if it takes mopping and baking to win back Robby Ray's approval, Jackson will put on an apron and get scrubbing.

FEEL THE BURN

Jackson has a knack for getting himself into a jam, whether it's getting snapped by mousetraps, tied up in one of Rico's contraptions, or burned to a crisp in the sun. But his real talent (or so he thinks!) is getting out of trouble. Too bad for Jackson, Robby Ray is hot on his trail!

BEST FRIEND

Lilly Truscott and Miley Stewart are the closest of friends. They have a lot in common: school, their beach neighborhood, and great times together. But Lilly also has a style that's all her own. She's a tomboy with a rad sense of fashion and a secret identity that lets her rock a totally different side of herself.

Funky hairdos are signature Lilly.

Lilly and Miley love dressing up for fabulous parties, but some of their favorite times are laid-back pajama nights at Miley's house.

TRUE FRIENDS

Even when their schedules are packed with concerts and soccer practice, these pals always find a way to squeeze in some Miley-Lilly time. They know they can always lean on each other!

FACTFILE: Lilly Truscott

Nicknames: Lilly Pad, Lil, Skater girl, Lil-lay

Catchphrases: "Eeeep!!," "Ooh! Lilly Likey."

Favorite things: Skateboarding, surfing

Secret talents: Playing soccer, doing flips for the cheerleading squad, faking a Swiss accent

Lola Luftnagle

TOP SECRET IDENTITY

At first Lilly wasn't comfortable glamming it up in disguise as Hannah Montana's friend Lola Luftnagle. But with wild-colored wigs and amazing outfits, she's learned to play her high-profile part in her own way. And it means she gets to spend lots of time with her best friend!

PARTY GIRLS

Once Lilly uncovered Miley's secret (by sneaking into Hannah Montana's dressing room), she became part of the Hannah action. She loves going to parties and interviews as Lola, and Hannah loves taking her…as long as she keeps her cool!

It's not easy keeping up with secret identities and a pop-star best friend, but even when Lilly and Miley (and Lola and Hannah) argue, they always make up in the end.

TROUBLE IN MALIBU?

Like any best friends, Lilly and Miley have their share of disagreements. But it never takes long for these two to remember that true friends are too important to give up.

"I think I'm gonna be sick. I need a fashion magazine! Cool, hip, trendy. Okay, all better!"

Lilly's acrobatics wow her friends and fellow athletes, and even win her a spot on the cheerleading team.

THE TOMBOY

Casual clothes are key for athletic Lilly, who likes to stay active and practically lives on a skateboard! Sure, she likes pretty shoes and funky accessories—but she's always ready to surf, skate, or kick back in comfortable style.

Sporty wristbands are skater-chic!

SMOKIN' OKEN

Oliver Oscar Oken is one third of BFF trio Miley Stewart, Lilly Truscott, and Oliver "Smokin'" Oken. He's been Lilly's pal since preschool, and quickly became one of Miley's most trusted friends, too. "OOO" talks a big talk with the ladies, but he's really a big softy at heart!

For Oliver, Miley's schemes can be messy work! He's even hidden in a trash can to record secret video footage.

Mike Standley the III

OLIVER TO THE RESCUE!

Loyal Oliver goes to great lengths to protect his friends. Whether it's going undercover as Officer Nancy or fighting off monkeys in Rico's locker, this shy guy finds the guts to step up when his friends are in trouble.

TOP SECRET IDENTITY

Oliver named his fricky-fresh alter-ego on the fricky-fly: he happened to see a microphone stand while introducing himself, and stammered, "Mike Stand-ley-the third!" Mike's look goes with his rapper persona: baggy clothes, hoodies, and hats worn backwards and sideways. The real secret behind his unique look: a goatee made of armpit hair!

LOCKER MAN

At school, Oliver Oken is known as "Locker Man" for his uncanny ability to open stuck lockers. What's in his? A sticky Blow Pop, pictures of cars, a note pad, a mirror, and, long ago, an eight-by-ten picture of Hannah Montana.

Shaggy-but-smooth hair says, "I'm wild, but I can be tamed!"

CASUAL COOL

With his shaggy hair, sweet smile, and cool, relaxed sense of style, Oliver is a boy-next-door cutie. "Smokin' Oken" takes the mike at games and dances and chats with all the girls—but at heart he's a sensitive guy with stage fright!

Pendants give Oliver's look a rocker edge.

ON THE AIR

You won't find Oliver on the court at gametime—he's behind the mike, with colorful commentary on every play! This AV whiz is also the DJ at school dances, and an amateur filmmaker who's a natural with a video camera.

With a tailored jacket, Oliver is dressed to impress!

FACTFILE: Oliver Oken

Nicknames: Smokin' Oken, the Ollie Trolley, Locker Man, the Triple O

Catchphrases: "Wiki-wiki-wa," "Fricky fricky fresh."

Likes: Girls, music, Hannah Montana

Secret talents: Keeping secrets, impersonating a fruit fly

RICO'S SURF SHOP

At Rico's Surf Shop, customers can get hot dogs, nachos, popcorn, soda, water, and even T-shirts and sunglasses…for a price! Rico is a tough businessman, but Jackson manages to keep things cool at the Surf Shop counter. It's the go-to hangout on sunny days at the beach.

These sunglasses are so hot, a pair was once stolen by a raccoon!

A Rico's T-shirt is Jackson's work uniform.

DID YOU KNOW? Rico imported sand from Costa Rica for the Surf Shop.

BEST SEAT AT THE BEACH

The lunch tables at Rico's have a sweet location: on the shady sand right next to a busy beach path. It's the perfect place to bump into friends while grabbing a bite, or to refuel after hitting the waves.

SAY "CHEEZE"!

Scheming Rico will do anything to protect his profits—even dress up as a baby to steal Jackson and Oliver's Cheeze Jerky recipe. If anybody's going to make money at the beach, he wants it to be him.

RICO'S TOP 5

tips for business success

- Trust no one
- **Protect the product at all costs**
- With advertising, the sky's the limit
- **Eliminate the competition**
- High prices=happy wallet!

At school, Rico's the youngest in his class. But what he lacks in years, he makes up for in sheer nerve! He's not afraid of a little blackmail and bribery to up his hall cred. Will he ever learn? True friends can't be bought!

"It's like taking candy from a baby."

RICO

The man behind Rico's Surf Shop is actually... just a boy! His dad may own the shop, but Rico runs the show. That means doing whatever it takes to keep his merchandise safe, his prices high, and his employees working hard.

Rico's confidence shines through in his smile.

FACTFILE: Rico

Nicknames: Shortstop, Mr. Irresistible

Catchphrases: "Mooahahahaha!," "It's Rrrrrrico!"

Favorite things: Money, Miley, practical jokes, embarrassing Jackson

Secret talents: Magic tricks, dancing, a photographic memory

FRIENDS & FRENEMIES

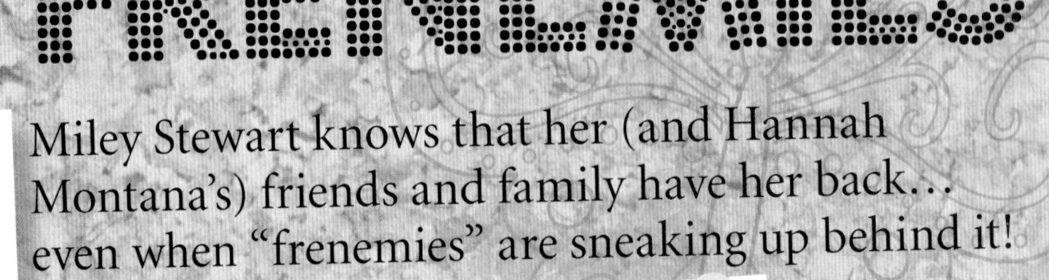

Miley Stewart knows that her (and Hannah Montana's) friends and family have her back… even when "frenemies" are sneaking up behind it!

Mamaw has wigs for every occasion.

Mamaw

Mamaw

Ruthie Stewart is Robby Ray's mom and a former Olympic volleyball player. But to Miley and Jackson, she's just "Mamaw"! Mamaw dotes on Jackson, but both her grandchildren mean the world to her. She visits them in California for big events, cheering them on at volleyball tournaments and awards shows.

Leslie "Jake" Ryan

Jake Ryan's starring role on TV's "Zombie High" makes girls all over school swoon. But he likes Miley because she was never swayed by his fame. Jake even tried his own secret identity to win her over—but the truth is, he loves being a celebrity!

Aunt Dolly

Miley enjoys hanging out with Jake…some of the time!

Jake

Aunt Dolly

When Miley's godmother Aunt Dolly comes to town, the house looks prettier, the air smells fresher... and disaster is never far behind. She has a way of causing trouble wherever she goes. But it's impossible to stay mad at Aunt Dolly, whose heart is as big as her hair!

Mikayla

Mikayla

Famous singer Mikayla and Hannah Montana have a pop-star rivalry that is friendly for the cameras, but off-screen the claws come out! Mikayla and Hannah make trading insults into an art form. Even Robby Ray and Mikayla's manager, Margo, get into the fray.

"Too bad you're not famous."

Ashley

Ashley's musical talent is limited to "snaps and claps."

Amber

Ashley Dewitt

Classmate Ashley can be friendly enough when she has something to gain, but usually, being nice is the farthest thing from her mind! She may not know much about friendship—or history, or geography, or Spanish, or music—but when it comes to being pretty and popular, Ashley thinks she's got it all figured out.

Amber Addison

Bossy Amber Addison rules the school with the help of mean-girl sidekick Ashley. She likes showing off her showstopping singing voice almost as much as spending her daddy's money, flaunting her good looks, and pushing around Miley and Lilly!

Traci Van Horn

Traci can usually be found backstage at Hannah Montana concerts, thanks to her dad the record producer. She's one of Hannah's biggest fans, and invites her to fabulous Hollywood parties.

Traci

SECRET KEEPERS

Hannah Montana has it all: killer clothes, adoring fans, first-class treatment everywhere she goes. The one thing she can't have? Peace and privacy to chill out and just be a kid. That's why Miley Stewart works so hard to keep her identity under wraps. If people knew her secret, Miley could kiss normal teenage life good-bye.

Miley Stewart will face any obstacle to help out the true friends who protect her secret. When Lilly enters a singing competition, Miley even braves a web of scary spiders to make sure her friend sounds as good as Hannah Montana.

THE OTHER SIDE

Unlike Hannah Montana, actor Jake Ryan has no problem milking his celebrity status. His fans give him tons of attention, but not much privacy or true friendship. Hanging out with him proved to Miley that her secret is worth protecting.

Miley is usually pretty careful about keeping her two worlds separate. But when they collide, it can take some sneaky solutions to repair the damage—including staging a photo shoot to keep the tabloids from finding out her secret.

Sparkling accessories make Hannah shine—and quick changes tricky!

LOLA MONTANA?

Desperate times call for desperate measures, like switching places with Lilly to impersonate Lola Luftnagle. But a simple switch is never simple! When Miley dresses as Lola, she winds up sharing a meal with the President's pooch.

"Sometimes it's nice to be treated like a normal kid."

Her blonde wig is part of Hannah Montana's disguise.

MEDIA ALERT!

Even Miley has trouble keeping her secret sometimes. She once spilled the beans to a reporter—but the Stewarts quickly covered with a truly terrible impersonation of Hannah Montana!

Glittery white and gold outfits make Hannah easy to spot in a crowd.

MILEY'S TOP 5

tips for keeping a secret

- Know who to trust
- **Don't talk in your sleep**
- Remember the details: Even the wrong accessories can give you away!
- **Avoid reporters at all costs**
- Know when it's time to come clean

SHHH DON'T TELL!

At first, it's scary for Miley to trust new people (even Lilly!) with her Hannah Montana side. But in the end, her family and friends are key to keeping Hannah hush-hush.

SECRET CLOSET

Miley Stewart is just a normal girl, with just a normal closet…right? Only a few people know the truth: Behind the walls of Miley's ordinary wardrobe is fashion Nirvana! Hannah Montana's closet is like a mini-department store—filled with red-carpet-ready clothes, shoes, bags, and jewelry fit for a teen queen.

DID YOU KNOW?
Hannah's fabulous shoes are all size five.

Miley and Lilly squeeze into a dress—at the same time!

MORE THAN A CLOSET

This is no ordinary closet. At the push of a button, racks revolve to show every outfit, and shelves of shoes and handbags roll out from the walls! There's even a comfy chair for chilling out between changes.

A raised platform rotates to bring every outfit into view.

HANNAH'S TOP 5

fashion tips

- Pick outfits that are easy to dance in
- **Use belts and scarves to spice up your look**
- Don't be afraid to change things up
- **Treat your clothes well**
- Find the look YOU love—and work it!

Alien Miley

Dressing as Hannah Montana isn't the only chance Miley Stewart gets to try new looks. She's been known to wear some pretty crazy costumes—for the right cause! Miley will even dress in an alien costume if it means outdoing her rival, Mikayla.

Queen of Style

Miley's style reaches new heights (and widths!) when she poses for Rico's art project. Who says a country girl can't conquer the world?

WHAT IF?

Miley Stewart works hard to keep her Hannah Montana side a secret. But sometimes she wishes she didn't have to go to all the trouble. Would it really be so bad if the whole world knew her secret? What would life be like if she could just be Hannah Montana?

STAR LIGHT, STAR BRIGHT

Leading a double life gets so complicated, it's sometimes hard to see the bright side. When Miley wishes on a shooting star, having just one life seems like it would be a dream come true. But would it?

Miley wishes to be Hannah all the time.

Lilly wishes for an A on their science project.

MAMA MIA!

A moonlit gondola ride with Jesse McCartney? That's amore! Finally, Hannah Montana can make plans with friends whenever and wherever —without checking with her dad or Miley's schedule.

EVIL STEPMOM

Candice schemed her way from celebrity tutor to pampered wife. Now she spends her time shopping, traveling, and doing whatever it takes to get her way. She's got Robby fooled—and wrapped around her mean little finger.

Chef Pierre presents Hannah's favorite breakfast: triple Dutch chocolate cake with a fudge ripple middle!

"You wished upon a star, now Hannah Montana is who you are!"

CRABBY HERMIT

Jackson lives on the beach searching for change and chasing away strangers rather than living at home with spotlight-hogging Hannah Montana. At least his dolphin friends listen to what he has to say!

POPULAR GIRL

Without Miley to help her be herself, Lilly drops surfing and skateboarding, and joins Amber and Ashley's pretty-girl clique. She wouldn't give a down-to-earth girl like Miley the time of day.

MILEY'S BACK!

Even Hannah's wish-life guardian angel is amazed when Miley manages to get her double life back. Everything is back to normal: Complicated, crazy, and just perfect.

Setting the stage for a jaw-dropping concert takes the support of a great crew. Each set has a system of stage props, lights, trapdoors, video screens, microphones, speakers, and special effects—and expert stagehands working behind the scenes to pull it all together.

The star dressing room is stocked with everything Hannah Montana needs before the show and between songs: Outfits lined up in order of appearance, the Hannah Box with her make up and wig, and a lighted mirror to check her finished look before she goes on stage.

Hannah Montana labels mark equipment for her show.

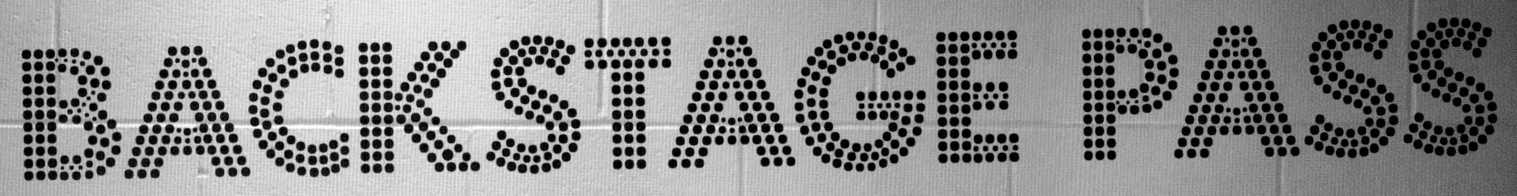

BACKSTAGE PASS

Being on tour means bringing everything—instruments, amps, speakers, lights, costumes, and even the set itself—to every arena. And that's just the beginning: Stagehands set the stage, technicians check the sound, and Hannah Montana gets her voice—and her look—ready to rock out the show. After the final bow, everything gets packed up again for the next stop....

Metal framework fits together on stage.

Amps and other sound equipment pull the band's sound together.

Trunks hold lights and projectors.

Heavy speakers have built-in handles.

DID YOU KNOW?

Hannah's tour bus has a full dressing room on board!

Getting ready for a concert doesn't all happen backstage. Before every show, Hannah Montana takes to the stage for dress rehearsals and sound checks. Hardworking Miley wants to get everything just right before the arena fills up, so she can give her fans a performance to remember.

Part of Hannah Montana's job is traveling for concert tours and charity events. That means Miley's got plenty of miles under her belt! In the middle of a tour, it's hard even to remember what city she's in—let alone slow down and enjoy the sites. Hannah Montana's logo shows some of the places she's performed.

Montana, the state that's Hannah's namesake.

Mooville, MN: Hometown of Jackson's friend Thor.

Loretta's Diner, where Miley's parents met.

Cawker City, KS: The world's largest ball of twine.

Malibu, California

Seaview High School, California

Life isn't all glitz and glamour—between the shows, Miley has to turn up for class in Malibu.

Los Angeles, California

It's not just Hannah who gets to experience the red carpet when Jake takes Miley to a film premier.

Lola claims that she is home-schooled in Canada.
Blue Earth, MN: 55-ft (16.8-m) statue of the Green Giant, champion of Niblets!
Washington D.C.
One of Hannah's biggest fans has the ear of the President! Seven-year-old first daughter Sophie lives with her dad, the President, and his dog, Humphrey, in the White House.
Cleveland, OH: Rock and Roll Hall of Fame.
New York, NY: New York Music Awards.
Audubon, IA: A 30-ft statue of Albert the Bull.
Mitchell, SD: Corn capital of the world.
Crowley Corners, TN: Miley's hometown.
Nashville, TN: Country Music Hall of Fame.
en-route to Florida
Lucky Miley gets to travel First Class to Hannah Montana award shows and charity events.
Hannah sang at the United People's Relief charity concert in Florida.
Hannah's concert tours take her all over the country.
Albuquerque, New Mexico

CALIFORNIA GIRL

Miley Stewart moved to California with her family when she was 10 years old. It's a far cry from Tennessee, but Miley soon feels right at home in Malibu. It's near TV and recording studios—perfect for Hannah Montana. And it's got a laid-back beach vibe that Miley loves.

Miley's surf-style is pure California.

CLASS ACT

Miley goes to Seaview High School, where she and her friends each find a way to shine: Miley is an A-student, Lilly scores big in sports, and Oliver mans the mike as a DJ and announcer.

Miley dances her way to an A in biology.

Miley is a good student, but even she needs some help with tough subjects. Remembering the names of 206 bones is a lot easier when they're set to music and choreographed!

HOUSE GUESTS

Miley's Malibu home is open to the ocean breezes…and to relatives in town for a visit! When the Stewarts can't go home to Tennessee, their relatives—and Miley's godmother, Aunt Dolly—bring a little bit of country to the West Coast.

MILEY'S TOP 5

things about living in California

- Tons of sunshine
- **The best shopping**
- Great views of the ocean
- **Warm weather all year round**
- Surfer dudes!

"You're in California now."

The best thing about beach life is…the beach! When it's time to take a break, Rico's Surf Shop is the place to grab a snack and some shade. Malibu beach can even be a great place to shop—for everything from shoes to handbags—when the flea market comes to town.

OUCH!

California is cool—but that doesn't mean Miley and Lilly don't get burned by pranksters. Practical jokes are a high-school tradition everywhere, and Malibu is no exception.

TABLOIDS SAY WHAT?

These girls love gossip. And in California—where celebrities and paparazzi are everywhere—there's plenty of it! But the news isn't always good: Hannah Montana freaks out on Rodeo Drive? It's in there!

When Robby surprises Miley by flying to Tennessee instead of New York, she can't believe her eyes!

Miley takes some time out from glamorous Malibu to reconnect with her roots when she goes back to her old home, Crowley Corners, Tennessee. The sleepy town takes a little getting used to after a few years away, but Miley soon remembers she's a country girl at heart.

Miley can rela
and be herself i
her hometown.

SMILEY MILEY

The people in Crowley Corners—and especially Miley's old friend Travis Brody—remember her best for her warm smile and pretty voice. Long before Hannah Montana recorded her first hit song, Miley loved making music with her family and friends.

Miley's acoustic guitar helps inspire her new music.

HARD WORK

Miley pitches in to help Travis build a new chicken coop at the farm. It's hard work, but seeing it all come together (and getting to spend time with Travis!) makes it all worthwhile.

FARM LIVING

When she first returns to Tennessee, Miley has a lot to learn about farm life—including how to feed chickens without starting a fine feathered riot! Anyone can dress the part, but learning to look after the chickens, gather eggs, and take care of her horse, Blue Jeans, like a real farmer takes some tips from the pros. (Hint: Let go of the feed bucket!)

MILEY'S TOP 5

things about living in the country

- Beautiful views
- **Galloping on Blue Jeans**
- Being close to family
- **Relaxing and being yourself**
- Remembering the simple things in life

FARMER'S MARKET

Grandma Ruby and other farmers sell their fruits, vegetables, and homemade goodies at the farmer's market. It's the best place to say "hi" to friends and neighbors. Miley helps out at the stall, cutting up watermelon samples and keeping an eye on Ruby's prize-winning vegetables.

LAUGHING PLACE

One of Miley's favorite spots in Crowley Corners is a beautiful hidden pond, complete with sunlight, wildflowers, and "jumpy rock." A rope swing she and Travis used as children is still there—and is still an exciting way to splash into the water!

THE CROWLEY CROWD

If anyone knows the real Miley Stewart, it's her friends and family back home. They're a little nuts, but they look out for each other through thick and thin. And they'll never give up on the hometown Miley they know and love!

Travis works on Ruby's farm.

TRAVIS BRODY

Travis Brody and Miley were childhood pals in Crowley Corners, but she barely recognized him as a cute 16-year-old when she went back home! "Cowboy" Travis reminds Miley how good it can feel to do a little hard work—and to spend quality time with friends.

Harlow can usually be found in Derrick's arms.

When cousins Miley, Derrick, and Jackson convene, Harlow the ferret is part of the mix. To animal-loving Derrick, he fits right in with family time!

"Nobody gets away with hurting my Miley."

Ruby is tough—but her heart belongs to her family.

Grandma Ruby looks sweet, but she'll put up a fight for her farm, her hometown, and her grandaughter Miley.

ALL TOGETHER NOW!

Hannah Montana may be used to thousands of fans cheering her on, but for Miley, Ruby, Robby, Jackson, and the gang in Crowley Corners, nothing beats the support of friends and family.

Miley kicks back with her family at the Save Crowley Meadows fund-raiser.

ANIMAL FRIENDS

In Malibu, dogs may be a man's best friend. But in Tennessee's wide-open spaces, there's room for all kinds of animals! And with a farm and a petting zoo, the Stewart family has quite a collection of animals. Keeping this creature crew in line takes some hard work—and sometimes some big bites! But life in Crowley Corners wouldn't be the same without them.

DERRICK'S PETTING ZOO

Cousin Derrick invites visitors to see his beloved animals at his roadside petting zoo. It's a small business with some very big assets—including an alligator, llamas, and an ostrich! Lucky for Derrick, he's got Jackson to help him keep them all fed and groomed.

Travis is a natural with horses. He takes care of Blue Jeans as part of his summer job at Ruby's farm.

Blue Jeans

Blue Jeans the Horse

Long before Hannah Montana rode in her first limousine, this beautiful gray mare was Miley Stewart's ride around Crowley Corners. It takes some time for Miley to remember how to gallop like she used to, but old Blue Jeans is one of the best things about coming home.

Miss Pearl

Miss Pearl the Alligator

The worst job at Derrick's Petting Zoo? Feeding Miss Pearl! Her nickname may be sweet, but the pearly whites she's named for are anything but. Miss Pearl is one of Derrick's most popular exhibits. Watching her powerful body swim and crawl is really amazing—and so is the mealtime tug-of-war with Jackson!

DID YOU KNOW?

Fully grown alligators can weigh up to 1000 pounds (455 kg). Look out, Jackson!

Harlow the Ferret

This furball has style! At the petting zoo, Harlow is Derrick's right-hand man. Derrick brings him everywhere—from casual family dinners to formal events—even if it means trying to keep him hidden away. But Harlow never likes to sit still if there's a party going on!

Harlow

The Ostrich

"You look different—you do something to your tail?"

The Ostrich

In the wild, ostriches can run faster than any other two-legged animal. At Derrick's Roadside Petting Zoo, this fiesty feathered gal prefers keeping Jackson on the run! She shows off for visitors by nipping at the hired hand, but with Derrick, she's sweet as a dove.

SAVE CROWLEY MEADOWS!

Crowley Corners owes its beautiful view partly to Crowley Meadows, the open countryside surrounding the little town. The land was left to the town in Mr. Crowley's will…but paying the taxes on it may be more than the residents can handle.

DID YOU KNOW?
Tennessee's state wildflower is the passion flower.

CROWLEY MEADOWS MALL

If the town can't raise enough money to keep the Meadows, developers will be only too happy to take over the prime real estate. Slick Mr. Bradley dreams of replacing the open fields with a huge shopping mall.

GET INTO THE ACT

At the Save Crowley Corners benefit party, everyone is invited to show their stuff on stage—including Miley Stewart! It's been a long time since Miley sang in public as herself, but when she does, she brings the house down with her "hoedown throwdown."

"It's for a good cause."

JUST THE WAY WE LIKE IT

The beautiful Meadows have always been a part of Crowley Corners' special charm. Sunlit, breezy fields filled with wildflowers and tall grasses are a perfect place to take a walk in the fresh air of the countryside.

Miley and Travis pitch in by pasting up flyers in town for the Save Crowley Meadows fund-raiser. Raising enough money to make a difference takes a little hard work from everyone.

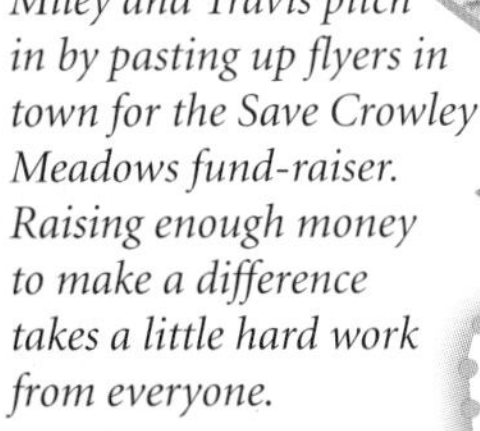

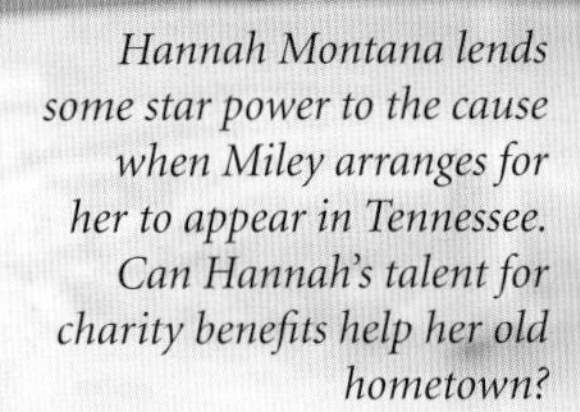

Hannah Montana lends some star power to the cause when Miley arranges for her to appear in Tennessee. Can Hannah's talent for charity benefits help her old hometown?

CROWLEY CORNER'S TOP 5

charity fund-raising tips

- Invite everyone to get involved
- **Get the word out with posters and flyers**
- Organize a fund-raising event
- **Bring in a big name to make a big splash**
- Never back down!

SWEET NIBLETS!

Miley's challenge in Tennessee is finding out how to be true to herself—and not get carried away with Hannah Montana's star status. She's got to learn to keep the glitz and glamour in its place: fourth in line after being true to herself, her family and friends, and her dreams.

NEW HANNAH

Spending time at home helps Miley find Hannah Montana's new style—including heartfelt songs and a rockin' wardrobe that lets her inner country-girl shine through.

A vest gets a Hannah-style makeover!

TOUGH MEDICINE

When Hannah Montana's diva side gets out of control, Robby Ray takes her home to Tennessee for a dose of reality. If Miley can't behave, it's good-bye to Hannah forever!

T-shirt and jeans are casual and cool.

CITY SLICKER

With a farm mural behind her and bales of hay underfoot, Hannah Montana kicks off the show in a slick suit vest that looks fantastic—but doesn't quite match her farm backdrop. Her backup dancers groove through their routine in business suits!

MILEY'S TOP 5

lessons from Crowley Corners

- You can count on family
- **Take care of your home, and it will take care of you**
- Hard work has its rewards
- **When in doubt, tell the truth**
- Always be true to yourself

"If it's not too late, I sure would like a second chance."

The songs are a smash as always, the backup dancers are rocking out, and the crowd is going wild...but Miley feels so guilty for letting down her family and friends that the unthinkable happens: Hannah Montana stops the show to give away her secret! It's a big sacrifice for Miley, but it feels good to come clean and ask for another chance with the people she loves.

Hannah Montana is used to her fans being supportive. But this hometown crowd loves Miley Stewart, too. Everyone agrees to keep her secret so Miley can keep living a normal life, and Hannah Montana can keep singing for all the world to hear.

LONDON, NEW YORK,
MUNICH, MELBOURNE, AND DELHI

Editorial Assistant Jo Casey
Project Editor Elizabeth Dowsett
Senior Designers Jill Clark, Lisa Sodeau
Managing Editor Catherine Saunders
Publishing Manager Simon Beecroft
Art Director Lisa Lanzarini
Category Publisher Alex Allan
Production Controller Louise Kelly
Production Editor Siu Chan

First published in the United States in 2009
by DK Publishing
375 Hudson Street, New York, New York 10014

09 10 11 12 13 10 9 8 7 6 5 4 3 2 1
HD176—01/09

Based on the series created by Michael Poryes
and Rich Correll & Barry O'Brien.
Hannah Montana: The Movie written by Dan Berendsen.
Based on characters created by Michael Poryes and Rich Correll
& Barry O'Brien.

The publisher would like to thank Jon Spaull
© Dorling Kindersley for kind permission to reproduce
the photograph on page 43.

Published in Great Britain by Dorling Kindersley Limited.

DK books are available at special discounts when purchased in
bulk for sales promotions, premiums, fund-raising, or
educational use. For details, contact:
DK Publishing Special Markets, 375 Hudson Street
New York, New York 10014
SpecialSales@dk.com

A catalog record for this book is available from the
Library of Congress.

ISBN: 978-0-7566-4536-6

Color reproduction by Alta Image in the UK.
Printed and bound in China by Hung Hing.

Discover more at
www.dk.com

Hannah Montana's blonde wig tops off her look.

It's all about that voice!

Bright, shiny leggings are totally rock star.